SPECIAL AGENTS

and other

STORIES AND POEMS

Evans

SPECIAL AGENTS

and other

STORIES AND POEMS

selected by Pauline Francis

An anthology of winning stories from
the 2010-2011 World Book Day Short Stories competition

VISIT OUR WEBSITE
www.evansbooks.co.uk
Evans

Published in 2011 by Evans Brothers Limited
2A Portman Mansions
Chiltern Street
London W1U 6NR

British Library Cataloguing in Publication Data
A catalogue record for this book is available from the
British Library

ISBN: 978 02375 44430

Editors:
Sophie Schrey, Bryony Jones
Designers:
Rebecca Fox, Evans
Jo Kennedy, Us2Design

FOREWORD

This is the first time I have selected stories and poems for the World Book Day/Evans Short Stories Competition. When the shortlist arrived, I was excited because I knew that you – the writers – would take me to places I could hardly imagine….

I was not disappointed. I've travelled to magical and mysterious worlds; to worlds past, present and to come; to worlds of horror and happiness. I've travelled by real trains and ghost trains. And I've flown, though not in an aeroplane.

How did I select the stories and poems for this book? All those on the shortlist had good plots and exciting characters that made me want to read to the end. And when I read them aloud, they had rhythm, without too many adjectives and adverbs.

So how? I waited… and waited. The stories that I liked best were the ones that I was still thinking about the next day… and the next… and I'm still thinking about them as I write this. For me, that's the secret of good writing.

A special mention? Yes – to Anna Wasse, aged 8, of Norwich High School for Girls. Her understanding of the thoughts of an older person in her poem, *Grandma's Bed*, was brilliant.

Thank you to all of you who entered the

competition and huge congratulations to the writers of this selection.

Keep writing.

Pauline Francis
Hertfordshire, 2010

ACKNOWLEDGEMENTS

Ten authors, two poets, twelve winners, 2500 schools and more than 3500 entries made this year's World Book Day Short Stories Competition the biggest and most successful yet!

We are delighted at the enthusiastic response to this competition, and impressed by the very imaginative entries, offering a rich variety of genres, from humour and dark tales to thought-provoking drama. We really appreciate the time and effort that go into each contribution, whether it is a story, poem or illustration, and hope that you enjoy reading these winning selections, primary and secondary, as much as we have enjoyed putting the books together.

The standard of writing was high, often outstanding – the judge's task was far from easy, but the final winners across the two age categories, ranging from 8 to 17 years old, deserve our heartfelt congratulations. Commiserations, too, to the runners-up – don't lose heart, remember that even the most successful authors weren't always published on their first attempt.

Many thanks to all the teachers and librarians who encouraged their students to take part and organised the entries; without your hard work this competition wouldn't exist.

A special thank you is due to the authors and poets who provided opening lines, and to their publishers. And to Pauline Francis who, for the first time, took on the difficult and unenviable role of Judge. Without Pauline, this competition would be an impossible task.

For all their hard work in helping to organise the competition, thanks go to Cathy Schofield of World Book Day, Truda Spruyt of Colman Getty and Jo Kennedy of US2 for the fantastic cover designs.

Keep an eye on www.worldbookday.com and www.evansbooks.co.uk for information about the next World Book Day Short Stories Competition.

Thank you
Evans Books

CONTENTS

'I watched her as she got off the train. Just as the doors were closing, she realised she'd left something behind...'

Dan Freedman

Special Agents

by Connie Burdett

I watched her as she got off the train. Just as the doors were closing, she realised she'd left something behind... She whipped around, her calm, brown eyes now flashing with panic. She tugged her fur-lined coat tightly around her and sprinted back through the doors, her golden ringlets tumbling behind her. Something about her made me suspicious. Following that instinct, I crept quickly behind her.

I found her rummaging under one of the seats. Suddenly she stopped, and her head turned like lightning to face me. Luckily, I had sensed what she was about to do and dived behind a pillar a nanosecond before she turned. It seemed she had found what she was looking for just in time. The whistle blew. The train started to move. She cursed and ran with her long, agile legs to the closed doors. Pushing the button impatiently, she gave a shout of glee when they finally opened. She jumped off the moving train and I quickly followed her. She stumbled as her feet hit the ground, but regained her balance almost immediately.

Straightening up, she began running again. I had to run flat out to keep up with her. Fortunately, I had some money in my pocket so that when she called for a taxi, I was able to jump in another and say, 'Follow that cab!' Wow, I've always wanted to say that. Right, back to the story. Her taxi stopped outside the office block that my dad works at and nearly caused a collision with us. 'Just pull up here mate,' I said, surprisingly calmly.

Watching the woman sprint into the office block, I took a moment to think about what she was doing. No time for that, I told myself and jogged after the mystery woman. On the way, I thought of my cover story, to use if necessary. I was going to meet my dad for lunch. My invisible brakes screeched to a halt as I spotted the lady talking to a man in the corner of the room. I snuck towards the wall separating their part from another and pressed my ear against it.

'…cannot afford to lose it again. You are being too careless.' It was the man speaking. He spoke in a harsh, commanding tone that suggested authority.

'I know, sir. I did not mean to. This incident will not happen again,' said the woman, regretfully. Her voice was throaty and deep. A distinctive French accent could also be heard.

Suddenly, I remembered something vital.

The thing that she had found under the seat had been a briefcase. I mean, how many beautiful French women carry around a very important briefcase? Deciding to investigate a little further, I quietly sat down at another computer and began to type, still listening to the conversation behind me. I had a hunch, so I might as well try it out.

'DGSE homepage,' I whispered to myself. My friends always called me a computer whiz. At last, that skill was finally coming into play. I knew how to hack into the DGSE's account. 'Aha, now, special agents' profiles.'

Now I had found what I had been looking for. In front of me was the complete list of all the DGSE's special agents and their profiles. Scrolling down, I was lucky that there were pictures of each and every one of the agents. Finally, my eureka moment had come. The DGSE is France's General Directorate for External Security ('Direction Générale de la Sécurité Exteriéure in French). This woman who I had been so intently following is one of its special agents. I took a look at her status. 'Access denied,' it clearly stated. 'Pass code needed.' I racked my brains to think of a possibility for the pass code. What about Agent? Huh, got it on the first go!

I scanned the computer screen and part of her status announced, 'In England transferring documents of theft of the Bank of England to

DGSE base in England.'

I sat back in my chair stunned. As I was doing this, I noticed a silence in the room next door. Then the scraping of chairs. She was leaving the office. The time had come to take drastic action. I speedily dialled 999 on my mobile and waited. I gave all the necessary details. The police were on their way. My only job now was to keep her from leaving the office. This was my only chance. I put on my best pouty face and shuffled up to the pair.

'Ex-excuse me. I can't find m-my Daddy.' I broke down into tears.

The beautiful lady stooped down so her face was level with mine. 'Oh you poor thing, I will help you find your Daddy,' she simpered.

I heard the scraping of tyres on gravel from outside. Just a couple more seconds and I would have her. A door slammed. The woman straightened up immediately.

'I'm sorry child, I am meant to be elsewhere,' she said.

'Not so fast,' I retorted.

Policemen were charging up the stairs. They immediately took away her briefcase and handcuffed her on the spot. One of them said,

'You have the right to remain silent.'

The rest of the story rolled out like this. The DGSE had been planning this robbery for months. The government had been expecting something like this to happen for a while. Little did they expect that an eleven-year-old girl named Connie would foil the robbery. Finally I had done something worthwhile.

Connie Burdett, aged 11
St. Catherine's Preparatory School, Surrey

The Carrier

by Angus White

I watched her as she got off the train. Just as the doors were closing, she realised she'd left something behind. She rushed back, banging on the doors, but nobody came to her aid. I sat on my bench, watching intensely as she continued to sob and weep. The green flag waved, a shrill whistle sounded and smoke erupted from the funnel on top, that was inadvertently disturbing the otherwise sleek, black, perfectly-rounded body of the many-bodied caterpillar, the exquisite circles of the legs revolving in perfect synchronicity, moving the monster ever forward.

I left my bench, my master's words echoing in my head: 'Make her welcome, we don't want her to be scared, do we?' as his wide grin spread across his warty face, illuminating his loose skin and the unnecessary number of lumpy chins.

As the smoke cleared, I saw some large suitcases, and a small cardboard box with a string and a label attached. And then, after I could see more, I was able to observe her face and smaller details. Her hair was black, long and perfectly straight, her lips were glowing almost red in the sunlight and her blue eyes, deep in thought, had welled up with tears. But her skin was what made her so beautiful; it was a pale honey colour and very slightly freckled, perfect little freckles of a delicate hue and it was otherwise flawless, full of health and the best part of it all was that it seemed to glow with a kind of innocence, despite her distress.

When she looked round, she was surprised to see me standing there, and I thought a little frightened.

'Where did you come from?' she asked.

'Why are you sneaking up on me?'

'I am not "sneaking up",' I replied. 'I'm taking you home. Mary Light is it?'

'Yes.'

'I thought so; I've been watching you. You are rich then are you? I haven't seen many of you evacuee lot coming out of the First Class carriages.'

I had been thinking other things that I dared not say, and I regretted saying this one, especially after she hung her head and ignored my query. This was the first time I noticed her tear-stricken cheeks with fresh drops raining down from those beautiful blue eyes.

'Come,' I said. 'Follow me.'

So I walked away, and, to my surprise, she came, walking eagerly, her mouth opening and closing like a fish, as if she wanted to shout something but couldn't.

We climbed into the first taxi, waiting outside the station. As it happened, it was a rather comfortable taxi, as the seats weren't falling apart, and they had some cushioning still in them. I had been given enough money to transport us 'home', and there was a panel to separate the driver's cabin from where we were sitting so we could talk in private.

After some hesitation, when it seemed she was inspecting me, she talked and talked, but the only thing I took any notice of was the reason she had been crying. She said it was something important, and something precious to her, but she would not, after many attempts, let out what it really was, or why it was important, not even who it was for or who told her to give it to them. But she did say that it had to be given to somebody by tomorrow, or the whole war that had lost thousands of men from our country was in great danger of being lost. By the time I reached my 'home' I had made up my mind, and I think she had too. So we pretended to walk into the drive, but instead hid behind the trees, and the bushy plants and shrubs, which had not been cut for years. My master was not rich, but had inherited this giant house from his father, which he could not afford to maintain and its once beautiful gardens were being reclaimed by nature.

As the taxi disappeared into the distance, we crept out, round the giant hedges, and out into my first taste of freedom, no master to tell me what to do, and for once I was in a team, not doing pointless work around a crumbling house being shouted at for my pains.

We slunk away, back the way we had come, and fortunately I had memorised the way just from two journeys and so we followed my memory. After hours of walking, and as the sky darkened to an evil grey, the clouds seemed to suck all happiness from the world, two shafts of light, like two large eyes glaring down, watching us. It was the Devil, I was sure of it.

I then heard the tired horn of another monster coming in, and we dashed down the road, stumbling over the dropped bits of debris, and finally we reached the station, just in time to watch the last train of the day roll down over the hills and into the glowering distance.

We had to stay away, as my master would beat both me and the perfect Mary, for he was not a kind man. Life would be tough, yet more comfortable for me because I could be free. Mary, however, was restless and unhappy. She was pacing round the station, banging on all the locked doors hoping for something, although I didn't know what. Whatever it was, her secret was deeper than I could imagine and more than she had told me. I felt as though my head was burning, just like when Master tried to burn me, just for the fun of it and, when I resisted, flogged me. He knew that he could achieve nothing from it other than his own pleasure; he seemed to enjoy other people's pain, living on it, feeding from it, just like the Devil.

I lay down on the cold stone floor of the station's waiting room and slept. I had no dream, just flashbacks of the past, living memories, tormenting me, the evil grin on my master's face as he stared in delight at my deeply scarred back, the slashes on my face, and the fresh blood trickling down my leg, face and side.

I do not know where Mary slept or whether she slept but it was still dark when she shook me awake and told me that there was a train approaching. She held two tickets in her hand and clearly expected me to board the train with her. I was meant to be looking after her but it seemed that she was looking after me and she could not have been more than fourteen years old. There was no plan that I could understand, although I know that she had to find the thing she had left on the train the evening before. I suppose that there was a place where lost property was taken to, back to the station in London.

The train hissed as it stopped at the platform and the doors opened. A tall man got out and went to sit on a bench under a sign with an arrow, saying 'Lost Property'. I followed the direction of the arrow and saw that it led to a hatch with the same words above it. It was closed.

We mounted the steps to the First Class carriage and I felt overwhelmed as she led me into the unfamiliar luxury of one of the compartments, which smelt of wood polish and lady's perfume. She sat down and I stood awkwardly, holding my old hat in both hands, until she pointed at the stuffed seat opposite her, indicating that I should do the same. The train stood for many minutes, making sounds like some wild beast and I felt nervous that somebody would come and tell me that I had no right to sit there. Mary was silent and seemed uncomfortable, frequently glancing out of the window at the tall man in the dark overcoat who remained seated on the bench in the station. It was as we sat there, without saying a word, that I heard the sound. Not the untamed sound of the train but a quiet noise of distress above my head.

Mary's eyes darted up quickly. She leapt from her chair and grabbed something from above my head, which turned out to be a basket, the sort which animals are sometimes carried in.

The animal, for that is what it was, mewed again, gently, and I saw Mary's eyes soften. Without a word, she leapt from the train and rushed over to the hatch marked 'Lost Property', which was just starting to open. She seemed agitated and after some excited arm waving, from both the young girl and the surprised old man on the other side of the hatch, she thrust the basket at him and walked away.

I was more nervous than ever, not knowing whether she would come back and again wondering about who was looking after who, and it was to my great relief that she turned back towards the train, just as the whistle blew, but this time she managed to reach the door before it closed and quickly climbed up the steps. As the doors slammed shut and the train started to move, I saw the tall man move casually from his bench to the lost property counter. The man behind the hatch passed him the same basket that had been in our carriage and he returned to his seat. He took out the cat, for that was what it was, and handling it quite kindly, he took off its collar and pulled out a small piece of paper from it. He glanced at it, then tore it in several pieces and threw it into a rubbish bin. Still carrying the cat, he walked from view.

I saw that Mary had also seen but she was silent.

What now? I was going to London but that was all I knew.

As though she understood what was worrying me, but speaking more to herself, she said: 'It will be alright now. We will go to my aunt. We will be able to live there.'

Not understanding anything and being both frightened and relieved, I just nodded and sat on my overstuffed seat, looking out of the window as we passed through places I had never seen, on my way to somewhere I could not imagine. Whatever should happen next, the child, Mary, was my new life and I knew that I would do whatever she asked.

Angus White, aged 11
Magdalen College Junior School, Oxford

'I said I didn't do it, but the truth is that I lied.'

Cressida Cowell

Freedom

by Helena Hughes-Davies

I said I didn't do it, but the truth is that I lied about keeping a girl in my wardrobe. I take her food; but not too much otherwise Momma gets suspicious. And this is what happened.

I sat on my white swing, white frock neat and straw hat straight. I rocked a little, listening to the birds. I could feel the grass tickling my feet, like a thousand feathers. Suddenly there was a great commotion on the street. Whistles were blown, maids shrieked and the milk boy dropped his bottles. There was one shot, no, two. I tensed and watched as a young black girl ran, panting slightly, up the hill. She wore a mustard-yellow dress, with an old, faded green pinafore. After further inspection, two figures in the distance trailed after her. Much to my astonishment, she calmly walked up the path towards me.

'Your momma wants you in the parlour, Miss,' she said loudly.

I looked bewildered.

'Just play along for a moment,' she whispered.

I understood she wanted me to do what she said, so I did. 'Alright, but bring me my tea at six.' Her face broke into a small smile. 'Yes, Miss.'

'And I expect you've ironed my dress.'

'Yes, Miss.'

The people all around who had been staring relaxed. I led the girl round the side of the house just as the two figures, policemen, arrived. The moment we were in the shelter of the tool shed, I hissed, 'What are you doing? Who are you?'

She sighed. 'My name's Esther. I lost my pass in town. I ran off and needed to hide. I'm sorry, shall I leave?'

'No!' I cried, breaking into my seven-year -old self. 'Come indoors, have a biscuit and we'll play dolls.'

Esther smiled and stood up. 'What's your name?'

'Diane,' I replied, and suddenly we were sisters, skin colour not mattering.

That was six months ago, and now I'm eight. Esther has knocked more sense into me than anyone in seven years. She lived in my wardrobe, but when everyone was asleep, she slept in my armchair. I took a bag to every meal, so I could pass it on to Esther.

'Momma, come on,' I pleaded. Momma was sitting, chatting to other women while knitting.

'One moment, Diane,' replied Momma, hugging me closer. I looked out of the window of the Knitting for Women Institute. Outside buses departed and policemen prowled. People bustled around, parting for a horse-drawn cart gliding past.

'… And only the other day the police searched our house. Looking for a young girl I think,' said Momma's friend.

My stomach did a private rollercoaster, followed by my heart.

'Yes,' agreed our neighbour. 'It'll be you next,' she added, gesturing to Momma.

'Esther, wake up,' I urged, reaching into the wardrobe.

'What time is it?' Esther asked groggily.

'Come on! We've got to leave, the police are searching for you. We're going to have to find your pass.' We rushed to the chilly outside. 'OK, where do you think you left it?'

'Let's try the market; I've already looked at home.'

We searched everywhere, between the stalls of fluorescent lemons and glowing oranges, knocking over sacks of dried pomegranate seeds. Later on, every step I took pulled down my bones. The darkness closed up on us.

'Is there anywhere to stay?' I requested.

'Under an awning,' was the only reply I got.

The light shook me awake. Or was it a thing, no, a person? A man! I pulled myself out of sleep. The man was getting quite close, so I looked around for Esther. She was skipping along with crusts (breakfast) in her hands. When she saw the man she frowned. He was wearing a damp shirt and he had a cigarette hanging out of his mouth.

'Who are you?' she questioned.

'The man who wants money for staying in my territory,' the man spat menacingly.

I reached for my bag, ready to hand it over.

'No, don't!' cried Esther. 'We have every right to be here.'

The man grabbed at my hair and yanked.

'Get off her, she's only eight,' added Esther. And she punched him in the stomach.

'No! Stop it!' I yelled. The rips, cries and scratches that followed were too nasty to talk about. Esther was a hard nut, but so was the man. Finally Esther stood up triumphantly, swollen lip and all. In her hand was her... pass!

'He steals them,' she explained, 'and sells them on.'

Still smiling I turned around to see Momma.

Tucked up in bed, Momma came to talk to me. 'It wasn't your fault darling. That nasty girl forced you.'

'Where is she?' I sniffed; Momma wasn't right.

'In a detention camp,' Momma soothed.

Two hours' brisk walk away later, I changed into some maid rags and slipped past the guards unnoticed. The smell of sour milk was overpowering in the cell. I unlocked the door and hurried Esther out into the night.

'Welcome to freedom.'

Helena Hughes-Davies, aged 10
The Perse Prep School, Cambridge

The White Wolf

by Peter Mumford

I said I didn't do it, but the truth is that I lied. If they had found out, I would have been banished from the pack. But you probably don't know what I'm talking about. Let me tell you. My name is Howl. I am a wolf – not an ordinary wolf, but a small, weak white wolf. I have also just committed a crime. In the annual caribou hunt, I killed the stag. It is the custom that the stag should be killed by my pack's alpha male, Growler. But I killed it. I didn't exactly mean to (although I might have momentarily contemplated it at some point).

I have always been bullied and abused because of my colour and size. It happens every day – and almost no wolf cares to prevent it. I was beginning to get more and more desperate as I thought of a way to solve my problem. I wanted to do something somehow to show the pack – and myself – that I was not a weak omega after all.

When the hunt began, I was put in my usual position: back-left-wing (to which no caribou would ever be foolish enough to come). But I didn't stay in that position; why would I? I crept sadly into a clearing. Suddenly the caribou came rushing towards me. The stag was right in front of me – so I leapt, on the spur of the moment. When the other wolves arrived, panting, into the clearing, tired out from chasing the caribou, they found me next to the stag. And then, of course, Growler came up to me for questioning. I lied – and they went away – but it changed my life forever.

The next morning, I was woken up from my sleep by loud voices calling, 'Where's the stupid omega now? Come out, Whitey.' I raised myself and scrambled out of my cosy circle of bracken, where I slept. Dawn light was filtering into the den and already, the pack was up, roaming around the clearing, talking to each other. And there they were – my tormentors, led as usual by Claws, a wolf of my own age.

'Well, if it isn't the runt,' he sneered. 'Had a nice sleep last night?'

He had put thorns in my bedding and they had hurt. I had spent almost the whole night getting them out of my fur. Before I killed the stag, I would have looked hurt and walked away, but now, I wasn't the coward I used to be. I marched up to Claws with a furious feeling inside me, but before I could say or do anything, he put out a paw and shoved me so hard that I fell over on my back. The others looked on with interest. Never before had Claws treated me as a potential adversary. Before, it had always been disdain and ridicule.

As I walked out of the forest to think for a while, I heard a loud voice calling my name. It was Pricket, a senior wolf in the pack and one of my enemies. He and his cruel mate Slick hated and despised me even more than the others for being a white wolf. 'Come here, Howl,' he yelped. 'You haven't cleaned out your bed of bracken.' But I had. Either Pricket was telling a lie or somebody had played a trick on me.

I soon found out what it actually was. Somebody had torn apart six bracken circles and, as usual, I got the blame. That's what I spent the rest of the day doing – repairing them. But I only finished half of them. I would do the rest the next day. I went to sleep that night feeling that I hadn't achieved anything by killing the stag.

However, the next morning, something happened in my favour. Claws and his gang were halfway across the clearing, so I gave them a wide berth. But a young member of his band kept following me. I didn't know how to shake him off. His fur was black – you'd think that black wolves would be persecuted like white wolves, but they're so common that no wolf thinks they're different. After five minutes of being followed, I finally decided to ask him to go away and leave me in peace but I never got around to saying that. As soon as I turned around, he introduced himself in a quick and excited voice.

'Hello – I'm Blackthorn. I wondered if you'd like some help with those bracken circles.'

I was taken aback. Almost no wolf had ever treated me kindly before. I said I would be very glad of his help. As we headed off to finish the tidying up, I knew I had made a friend.

Amazingly, things started to take a big turn for the better after that. Blackthorn's popular sister, Whisper, who had patches of white amongst her grey-black fur, warmed to me after her brother became my friend. Whisper's friends began having different views about me – and they had friends… so, soon, most of the pack did not look on me with disdain anymore – apart from Claws, Pricket and a few others. But it didn't last for long.

The pack had been having many problems since even before I was born. There was danger from lone wolves outside the pack and bears. Even worse threats came from humans; they had taken away my parents in their traps. The pack felt itself getting weaker than it had been. Pricket decided to take advantage of the situation. He said he could make the pack strong again. In his opinion, Growler was a soft and undisciplined leader who would do nothing to prevent the pack's decline.

He didn't say that to Growler's face, though, but he and Slick went around the camp whispering it into wolves' ears. He then persuaded the wise and just Growler to resign as alpha male so that he himself could take over. The pack was tired of being weak and willing to go along with anybody who promised good fortune. And so, the happiest point in my life was very short-lived.

'As alpha male, I pass a new set of rules to you,' said Pricket. 'The first is that we must have no weak wolves in the pack.'

'When you say "weak wolves",' piped up Claws, 'do you mean white wolves?'

Whisper gasped and rolled in the dirt a bit more to disguise her patches of white fur.

'You are exactly right, Claws,' replied Pricket. 'The surest sign of a weak omega wolf is pure white fur, which means…'

All heads turned and looked at me. I had a sinking feeling of dread at what Pricket was going to say next.

'… Howl, you are banished from the pack.'

I was outraged. I turned to the pack. 'You can't just let him banish me,' I exclaimed. 'What have I done to deserve this treatment?'

'Lots of things,' smiled Claws.

I was horrified. The pack was agreeing with him. I saw a few nodding heads and then, a chant of, 'Banish him, banish him, banish him…'

Out of the crowd of wolves came a lone voice, 'Don't banish Howl. Get rid of Pricket instead!' But Blackthorn's words were lost in a tide of rage. I didn't want the rage to become physical, so I turned and slipped out of the camp, glancing at Blackthorn's sad face as I did.

As I padded away from the place I had called home ever since I was born, my thoughts were in a jumble: sadness and anger at Pricket, and worry about what would happen to me. Would I die? Join another pack? Or stay a lone wolf, abandoned and hated by all? By nightfall, I had found a small hollow of moss and leaves, just outside my pack's territory. I was too exhausted to go on, so I slept there. In the morning, I woke up thinking, Where am I? Then I remembered. That day was horrible. I caught a hare to satisfy my hunger and returned to the hollow, only to find it inhabited by a stoat. We had a fight – stoats are surprisingly strong and very tough – and in the end, it won. I was driven out of my shelter, for the second time.

I wandered hopelessly over the hard, rocky ground, looking for anywhere that might be a resting place. It was then that I heard the first howl. Coyotes! They had never gone near my pack, but they might attack a wounded young wolf out on his own. I crouched behind a tall rock, hoping they wouldn't see me. I saw eight or nine shadowy shapes prowling around the rock. I snarled, but they seemed to sense that I wouldn't be able to defend myself for long and they resumed their prowling. This went on for some time and finally, I decided that I wasn't a coward and I was going to face them. I stood up and ran at the nearest coyote, chasing him off into the darkness. I growled at the second one who took a pace back. Then, I heard a noise behind me and realised that I had been unvigilant. In a heartbeat, the third coyote had me on the ground. Now I knew I wasn't going to survive this encounter.

Suddenly I heard a yelp behind me and out of the corner of my eye saw a fleeing coyote. Then the weight on my body lifted and I staggered unsteadily to my feet to see someone I never thought I would see again: Whisper, with the coyote by the tail! She dropped him and he fled howling into the night. I bared my teeth, expecting a fight, but there were no more coyotes left; they had all run away. I turned to Whisper.

'Thank you ever so much for saving my life,' I said. 'How did you come to be here? Where's Blackthorn?'

'It's a long story,' said Whisper. 'Blackthorn couldn't come because he's already in trouble for being one of your friends. Slick has been going around the camp finding out who was friends with you and she and Pricket have been trying to convince them to renounce their friendship.

I'm sorry, but I said I hated you when Slick asked. I'm worried about Blackthorn. He said he'd never be disloyal to you and I'm afraid of what Pricket might do to him.'

That speech worried me a lot, but then Whisper said that most of the pack secretly opposed Pricket's decision to exile me and would prefer to have Growler back as alpha male now that they had seen what Pricket was really like.

For the next week, life was better, as Blackthorn or Whisper came every day with news of the pack and sometimes food, although I almost always rejected it because I didn't want to be dependent on them. One day, Blackthorn arrived with a rather alarming question. He asked me if I would come back to the pack's camp. I said that I couldn't possibly because Pricket had banished me, but then he told me that the pack wanted me back – even Claws. I was astonished. I almost didn't believe him. But I agreed to come with him the next day.

After all that time in exile, I had almost forgotten what the camp looked like, but I soon remembered. The pack was waiting beneath the big rock. I didn't know what would happen next. I half expected wolves to attack me but the look in the eyes of every wolf was one of friendship and kindness. Then, some wolves began cheering. Growler stepped out of the throng of wolves.

'We're very pleased to have you back, Howl,' he said. 'We apologise for supporting Pricket.'

Suddenly, a yelp sounded from the camp entrance. It was Claws. Every head turned and looked at him. He was exhausted and panting for breath. 'It's Whisper,' he gasped. 'Pricket's trying to kill her because he found out she helped Howl to get back here.'

Instantly, I sprang up and raced into the trees, following the waving tail of Claws. We burst into a small clearing to find Slick pinning Whisper to the ground. Before she had time to turn around, I leapt on her and pushed her off Whisper. She retreated, snarling. I heard a yelp from Claws that was sharply cut off. I had a feeling someone was creeping up on me. Then, a heavy shape knocked into me and everything went black.

When I came to my senses, Whisper was bending over me, pressing some wet moss to my stinging ear. 'What happened?' I asked.

'I haven't got time to tell you,' said Whisper. 'Claws is hurt too and I have to get him back to camp. Just go down to the lake. Pricket chased Blackthorn there.'

'But…' I began, wondering what Blackthorn had to do with it all.

Whisper cut me off. 'Blackthorn's in danger. Run!'

I pelted down to the lakeside, following the

trail of smashed bracken. I arrived, breathless, on
the shore, to find Pricket backing Blackthorn up
to the lake edge. 'You foolish omega! Why did you
help the white wolf?'

'Because I wanted to,' replied Blackthorn with
his head held high even though he was scared.

'Right,' snarled Pricket. 'Then you'll die here.'
He leaned forward and pushed Blackthorn into
the deep part of the lake. Blackthorn floundered
about for a few seconds, then regained himself
and swam strongly for land.

'I never expected that,' growled Pricket.
'Must I get into the water to ensure that you
die?' He turned and jumped into the water after
Blackthorn. Now Blackthorn was terrified. He
swam back into the deep water with Pricket
close behind. There was a rock sticking out of the
water. Pricket jumped onto the rock and used his
powerful hind paws to push himself right onto
Blackthorn's back.

I was about to leap in to the water to help my
friend when I heard a rustle in the bushes and
turned around to see Slick. 'What are you doing
here, Omega?' she spat.

'Trying to help my friend,' I replied in as calm
a voice as possible.

Then, she glanced at the lake which we had
both momentarily forgotten. 'Pricket!' she howled,
a howl of dismay. I turned to see Blackthorn

swimming into shore with his fur ruffled and wet. There was no sign of Pricket.

As Blackthorn dragged himself out of the lake, he gasped, 'I tried to save Pricket when I realised he was in trouble but I was too slow.'

Pricket had probably been the most evil wolf in the forest, but being the wolf I am, any death was sad for me.

'You killed my mate!' yowled Slick and dashed towards us, her teeth bared. Suddenly, like ravens flying silently through the trees, the pack arrived, seemingly melting out of the forest. It was Growler.

'When we accepted you into our pack, we believed you to be a loyal and trustworthy wolf. You have proved us wrong. With your schemes and lies, you have taken the pack over. You are just as bad as Pricket and therefore, we cannot let you stay. You will leave here and swim across the lake to the conifer forest where, I am sure, there will be another pack which will be foolish enough to take you in. Now go!' And Slick did go. She sprinted away like the wind.

Back at the camp, the pack gathered beneath the big rock and soon, Growler bounded up on top of it. 'Pack! I have some announcements to make. First, all the rules that Pricket made are now abolished. I would also like to make a new rule. From now on, all persecution, abuse and

discrimination against white wolves is illegal.'
I couldn't believe my ears. The pack crowded
around Growler, cheering. He pushed through
the crowd until he was standing right next to
me. He quietly whispered in my ear, 'I've been
watching you as you grew up. You have had a
hard and unhappy life, but you have risen above it
to become an honoured member of the pack. You
would be a worthy successor to me when the time
comes.' Then, he slipped into the shadows.

I gazed around, feeling puzzled, but everyone
else was looking beyond the camp to the snowy
plains of early winter. 'Look!' said Blackthorn with
a surprised expression on his face. 'It's the caribou!
They've come again!' And we were off.

Peter Mumford, aged 10
Sidcot School, North Somerset

'*Don't touch!* That's what the sign on the ancient Chinese vase read, but I couldn't stop myself reaching for it.'

Chris Bradford

The Lady of the Vase

by Imogen Parsley

Don't touch! **That's what the sign on the ancient Chinese vase read, but I couldn't stop myself reaching for it**, and when I did it felt cold and smooth. I leaned in a little closer to see the shapes of people in a small, ancient Chinese town. Suddenly the shapes started moving. The people were walking, talking, eating and drinking. It was amazing how a small vase in a small shop down the road from our house could do this and that's why I'm writing it down. Because maybe in the distant future someone will read my tale and find the vase where our home once was.

Well, I begged my mum for that vase but she just said, 'I'll think about it,' and when adults say, 'I'll think about it,' it almost always means no!

But luck was on my side because it was my birthday in two weeks and Mum knew I didn't want the same woollen jumper I get every year (twelve-year-olds aren't normally interested in woollen jumpers anyway!). So I just waited and waited for two weeks, going to the shop and looking at the vase whenever I got the chance.

When my birthday finally came around I opened my presents one by one. Dad bought me an encyclopaedia, Auntie Sue bought me a pair of trousers and Mum bought me... the ancient Chinese vase! I was so pleased that I decided to put it on display for when Grandma and Granddad came round for birthday tea. But I knew that if I put it on the display cupboard my little brother Jack would knock it off and I might have never seen it again so I put it in the trophy cabinet instead.

At six o'clock Grandma and Granddad came around for tea. They brought me an art set and a box to put my special things in. I said, 'Thank you so much, the box is perfect to keep my vase in and I do love art a lot!'

For tea we had Indian (my favourite!) and for pudding we had blackberry crumble (delicious!).

From then on I checked the vase every day. I always watched it first thing in the morning and as soon as I got home from school. Every day, just as the sun was setting in the ancient Chinese world of the vase, I would see a little old lady sitting on the floor with a handful of corn just in case a nightingale may pass, and if one did it would fly onto the little old lady's arm, eat some corn, rub its face on the little old lady's cheek and finally fly up to the old tree and sing its song for the little old lady who would be smiling the whole time!

One day, when I was staring into the vase, I noticed the little old lady wasn't there. I wasn't worried of course because she might have just caught a cold or got the flu or maybe had gone away to see her family. But after a while I started to wonder where she was so I got the vase out of the box to have a look and guess who I found sitting in the vase? The little old lady herself!

She spoke Ancient Chinese and she was only the size of a doll from my cousin's playhouse. I lifted her from the vase and held her in my cold hands. I knew she was so delicate and I couldn't be rough with her so I was extremely careful. Suddenly Mum shouted, 'Come on Lizzy, time for school,' and without thinking I dropped the little old lady into my schoolbag.

That day I did Science, English, Maths and Art at school. I gave the little old lady a piece of string and some buttons to play with and they seemed to do the trick. She was quiet all day until hometime when a small spider climbed into the bag and she screamed until I put it outside. Poor spider having to put up with that racket!

After school I went to the library. The little old lady pointed to a book called 'Beautiful Flowers'. I took it down from the shelf and flicked through the pages. It was full of pictures of flowers but my favourite picture was of a lovely sunflower! I gave the book to the little old lady and she smiled, looking at pictures of roses and daisies (but to be honest, I didn't really like flowers at all!).

At dinnertime I gave the little old lady some bread and cheese to eat and at bedtime I gave her milk and biscuits before tucking her up in the spare room.

One day the little old lady looked through a small hole in the vase. I watched her and looked through as well. Through the hole I saw the ancient Chinese town!

I decided to carve the hole a bit bigger so the little old lady could climb back to Ancient China. I took my carving tools and lay there carving away with the little old lady sitting on my bed. Suddenly Jack ran into the room and shouted, 'Boo!' I jumped and the vase flew out of my hands, breaking into tiny little pieces on the floor. I started crying but stopped when Mum shouted to me from downstairs. I grabbed the little old lady and only then I realised the walls of the house were crumbling and the roof was falling in. I ran out of the house with the little old lady in my pocket and stood outside with Mum, Dad and Jack, our home collapsing.

The remains of our house were flattened to

the ground and we rented a flat until our new house was built on top. Maybe, one day, that house will fall too and someone will dig so deep that they find the remains of my vase and maybe even discover its secret.

Imogen Parsley, aged 10
Ysgol Licswm, Flintshire

The Warrior from the West

by Charlie Longford

***Don't touch!* That's what the sign on the ancient Chinese vase read, but I couldn't stop myself reaching for it.** The ancient terracotta artefact was lava orange with Chinese language inscribed onto it. It featured historical battle scenes with Samurai warriors fighting for victory. As my finger drew ever closer to touching it, I noticed one warrior with silver and gold armour. He was brandishing a huge, curved blade – this was the warrior Tene Kahn. Some think of him as the most powerful and destructive warlord ever to have walked this earth. In any pictures of Tene his eyes would be found full of rage and hate. He was most famous for the occasion when he got so angry laying waste to the centre of Japan that he slaughtered everyone he could find and turned every building to flames.

My finger slowly pushed forward until it

touched the vase and as this happened I heard a thousand ghostly voices whispering to me, tempting me to release them. With these words burning and drilling into my mind, suddenly a flash of light blinded me and everything started spinning. Suddenly, BOOM, I was knocked off my feet. Then silence.

When I regained consciousness I thought I was going to see stars but instead I heard screaming, shouting and screeching in pain. I saw balls of fire whoosh past and fly overhead. I realised I was in the battle that was pictured on the vase. Luckily I was on Tene's side and I recalled from my history lessons that we had learnt about Tene's Battle of the Dark Hilltops. I remembered that was when Tene had fought his last battle because of an unknown supposed blunder that he had made. The terrible truth started to dawn upon me – this was in fact the Battle of the Dark Hilltops and I remembered Mr Oaks, the history teacher's words: 'At sunset Tene's fifteen-year reign ended after his army were slaughtered by the Japanese rebels.'

It was almost sunset now and there was still no sign of Tene. Suddenly a flaming arrow darted over from the rebels and came flying down at a breakneck pace. No doubt it could have mortally wounded me but just as I thought everything was about to end, a graceful but strong figure threw me out of the way. The arrow skimmed my head, singeing one half but because my hair was drenched with sweat it was not set alight. I could make my rescuer out more clearly now. He was a young man who looked about twenty. He smiled with tenderness and caring eyes. Although I did not even know his name, he felt like a friend. I had never had a friend before and for the first time in a while a smile began to form on my face.

As I got up I heard the faint sound of a horse's hooves. Rapidly one horse turned to tens of thousands – they sounded like thunder and then suddenly stopped. I turned around only to find the notorious Tene Kahn glaring piercing daggers into our eyes. Tene did not say anything nor did he need to because the sick smile he had displayed on his face and his two-metre sword said it all. He waved a finger and muttered something to what looked like his right-hand man. The man, who appeared to be a general, screamed something in Chinese. A few seconds later I found out that it was probably a war cry because a group of foot soldiers, who looked to be elite, grabbed us both by the scruff of the neck and dragged us over to Tene.

Tene looked at us in disgust. 'Tiresome rebels,' he said viciously. My friend whimpered in fear. Tene focused his eyes on mine as if he was trying to scare me mentally and then he said, 'Do you not fear death?'

I wanted to stand up for myself but then I realised this was not like being bullied in the playground – this man could end my life in a matter of seconds. He repeated the question,

'Do you?'

I still said nothing and my heart felt like it was on fire.

'Kill the timid one first,' he said and then he pointed at me. 'Let him watch his friend fall then kill him too.'

The general and his guards seized me and bound me to a wooden stand. They only bound my arms, not my legs and my left hand was only bound loosely so I could wriggle it free. However I tried to make them think I was still tied up so they were not suspicious. Suddenly my attention was drawn to Tene as he drew his lethal weapon and screamed, 'I hope the Japanese rebels see this because this will happen to all of them eventually.'

Infuriated, I went red in the face, a rush of adrenaline filled me and I put all of it into my legs and lashed out at the guard with one foot and with my other foot I knocked the crossbow out of his pocket so it landed right in front of me. My left arm broke free and I grabbed the guard by the throat, hurling him off the edge of the cliff.

Tene took aim for his first blow and as he lifted his arm a small hole in his armour was revealed on his chest. Mad with anger I managed to take the ropes off my arms and as the sword descended onto my friend I lifted the crossbow and fired the bronze arrow straight at the hole in Tene's armour. In pain he fell over, landing on his own sword. While the army were recovering from the shock my friend and I scampered off to safety.

Weirdly lights started flashing around me and everything started spinning and my friend's voice whispered in my ear, 'You have done well, you may now return.'

Suddenly there was a big bang and I had returned back to the vase shop with the vase right next to me. At first I thought it must have been a hallucination but then I heard the faint galloping of horses' hooves going clip clop, clip clop….

Charlie Longford, aged 10
Hall Grove School, Surrey

'"There is no such thing as *magic*," said Emma's mother.'

Daisy Meadows

There's no such thing as magic

by Felix Ross

'There is no such thing as *magic*,' said Emma's mother. And, 'Poof!' she disappeared in a puff of green smoke.

'That'll teach you,' chuckled Emma as she tucked the wand into her bag and headed off for school.

It was only a couple of days since old Uncle Wilfred had left her the wand in his will. He had died of a mysterious illness in Africa, apparently. But not half as mysterious as the wand itself. It obviously had magical powers, no matter what Emma's mum said.

How else had she managed to get through her fractions homework in double-quick time? Everyone knew she was hopeless at maths. How else did her cello practice suddenly sound so good? Even the dog had noticed. He usually ran out of the door whining the minute she picked up her bow. But last night was different. Everyone sat up and listened. With a flick of the wand, Emma's playing was transformed. For once, it actually sounded like music, as Mum grudgingly had to admit.

There was no doubt about it. This was magic. Since she got the wand, just about everything had changed. And with Mum out of the way for a few hours, Emma was looking forward to a very exciting day.

First up was assembly. Emma had always hated the way they were made to stand to attention every morning. Rows and rows of children like a bunch of wooden soldiers, or a stack of dominoes. The bumbling headmaster was already up on stage and had begun another boring address when suddenly – that was it!

With a flick of her wrist, Emma made all the dominoes topple over. From one end of the hall to the other. Clickety-clack-clickety-clack.

From Form Three to Form Eight, legs and arms and schoolbooks went flying as everyone bashed against one another and got their knickers in a twist. The chaos was wonderful.

Emma smiled to herself. Wow, she thought, this is magic.

Unfortunately, the effects didn't last. Everyone had recovered in time for morning lessons, and that meant only one thing: double science.

Emma soon realised there was lots of fun to be had with the Bunsen burner. First, she made it dance like a blue genie in front of the class. How they all 'ooh-ed' and 'ahh-ed' as the flame spun and twirled. She made it perform amazing pirouettes like they'd never seen before. The teacher, Mr Bognay's jaw just dropped. For once, he looked up from his textbook, muttering something about this, 'definitely *not* being on the curriculum.'

Then he singed his bushy eyebrows on the flame as it retreated into the burner. The whole class dissolved into giggles. This was great! Emma decided to go the whole hog. She turned the burner into fireworks, spouting all the colours of the rainbow. The lab was a mass of sparks! It was spectacular! It was magic – and it still wasn't even break time.

Next up was sport.

Emma was almost as bad at games as she was at maths. Every lesson began with a compulsory sprint around the field. Emma had never seen the point. Why wear yourself out before the lesson even began? She was usually the one coming in last, though she never thought this was much of a problem as she never got picked for a team. Today was going to be different. Emma grinned as Mr Ship sucked in his tummy and gave the starting orders.

'Ready! Set! Go!' And off she went. Just a touch on her wand and she was flying.

Everybody stared in amazement as Emma sped round the field like a cheetah and returned to the start. 'Shall I do another lap, Sir?' she asked without even panting. 'To give the others a chance to catch up?'

Mr Ship leaned forward for a closer look. His stomach sagged and he sank onto the nearest bench in shock. 'Yes, of course, Emma,' he sighed. 'Be my guest.'

Back in the changing rooms it was nearly time for break. Emma hadn't had this much fun for ages. She was just packing away her kit when she caught sight of a pair of the school's PE pants. She hated those PE pants with a vengeance! Huge and baggy, she had to wear them under her skirt for sport.

With a cheeky grin, and a flick of her wand, Emma knew just what to do.

Forty pairs of PE pants suddenly came to life. They flew around the cloakroom like large floppy bats. Dive-bombing the lockers, spinning on the hooks and landing – plop! – on people's heads. The screams were magnificent. Emma's joy was complete when a particularly large pair landed on Mr Ship's balding head and covered his eyes.

'Ahhh!' he cried in a terrified voice as he took

off down the corridor, 'I can't see!'

The rest of the morning went well. Everyone was thrilled when the French teacher, Monsieur Morton, conducted the whole lesson in Japanese and finished with his own personal karate demonstration. Geography was even better when Mr Muse himself became a living volcano, providing a perfect example of the stages of eruption they had been studying for weeks. It's true, Emma did feel a little remorse when his face turned bright red and flames shot out of his nostrils. Geography was her favourite subject after all, but even 'volcanology' needs livening up sometimes.

At last it was time for lunch.

Emma knew this would be her finest hour. As everyone lined up in the canteen, carrying their plastic trays, they knew just what lay before them. Soggy sausages with greying mashed potato and gravy that sat in a lump on the plate. Emma quite liked sausages and mash really. But not at school. It was the thick skin on the gravy that she could never really get used to.

Out came the wand and in a flash the sorry school dinners were transformed into a fabulous feast. Roast chicken with all the trimmings, stuffing, potatoes and crispy veg. For pudding there was chocolate mousse, strawberries and ice-cream. The canteen lighting turned to glowing candles. The dinner ladies, dressed in proper waitresses' uniforms, came smiling to the tables carrying dish after dish under huge silver platters. Everyone was happy. Emma smiled to herself as she looked at her friends' smiling faces.

The transformation of school lunch was complete.

In Design Technology, Emma designed a spacecraft and constructed it all from egg boxes and toilet rolls in under thirty minutes. With the aid of her wand she was able to add a few 'technological advances' and, much to the amazement of the teacher, she had a fully working aircraft by the end of the period. This, she put to good use during her final lesson – Music.

Emma had always liked Music. Mr Boyser was extremely enthusiastic and had done his very best this term to bring Holst's 'The Planets' to life. But Emma felt sure it would be so much better if they could actually see this amazing solar system for themselves. In real life, so to speak. Mars, Venus, Mercury – they were all out there waiting.

Just a flick and a swish of the wand, and the whole class was on board Emma's cardboard spacecraft. Within minutes they were in outer space. There, Mr Boyser was in his element, scarcely knowing which planet to show them next. Jupiter, Saturn, Uranus…. With Holst's music soaring in the background, it was the most wonderful field trip the class had ever had. Time magically stood still. Emma landed in the playground before the end of the last period. Everyone was chattering excitedly about all that they had seen. She put her wand safely into her bag and smiled to herself as she headed to the bus stop.

Her mum was there to meet her when she got home.

'Hello, dear. Did you have a nice day at school?' she asked.

'Yes, Mum,' Emma smiled. 'It was magic.'

Felix Ross, aged 10
New College School, Oxford

Northern Lights

by Hannah Erlebach

'There is no such thing as *magic*,' said Emma's mother. Emma felt as if the world was crashing down on her.

'Wh-what do you mean?' she stuttered.

'Exactly that,' said her mother grimly.

'But… that can't be! What other explanation can you find for luck and coincidence? Why do the clouds above us form distinctive shapes? And if there was no magic… what would become of the Realm of True Owls?' Emma posed determinedly.

Her mother gave her an affectionate peck on the shoulder.

'Emma, you are no longer a naïve young owlet. It's time that you should accept this. There is no so-called 'Realm of True Owls'.'

Emma listened in dismay as her mother continued.

'It's just a myth, sweetheart, this 'owl haven' does not exist. But don't fret; there, there settle down now. We've got another long night ahead.'

Emma obediently took her place on the branch, too dumbstruck to object, and shut her eyes tight. But before she embraced the velvety blackness of sleep she promised herself one last thing: 'I will find the Realm of True Owls; I *will!*'

Emma was jolted awake by a thud that propelled her straight into the air. Blinded by the streaming sunlight, she hopped under a cluster of pine needles and observed the scene below her from her new vantage point. The foliage rustled beside her as her mother descended swiftly on her left.

'Emma, have you seen that *repulsive* creature at the bottom of our tree? It has pinched pink skin without a trace of fur except on its head; it has four limbs but only walks on its hind two, like a bear does when it's angry; and it's carrying a big pole with a massive blade at the end! *And it's hacking straight at our-*' Both owls were flung into the air again as a result of another thud... '*-tree!*' she yelped.

Emma stationed herself between two sprays of pine, peered through the gap and almost fell out of the tree. A hideous, weathered creature stood underneath her own feet, its fluffed head almost brushing Emma's feathers. As she watched, it drew the blade and stabbed the tree once more. It was all Emma could do to stop herself screeching in apprehension. The one thing she would most happily have done at that moment was to deposit her waste on the creature's furry head… what an artistic splodge of black that would add!

But her instinct restrained her; and she managed to sit rigidly. That was when she heard a creak – and a groan – and she felt the tree bowing beneath her. A crack of tension tingled up her spine as the tree tendons delicately snapped one by one. She felt herself being pitched forwards like a rock on a landslide. She slid down the rapidly descending branch with an ear-piercing scrape of friction. In a flurry of feathers, she dodged the toppling tree and shot up into the sky, her mother close on her tail.

A dull reverberating thump almost knocked her clean out of the air. Emma winced as the once majestic pine clattered to the ground in a disgruntled heap of splinters. Plumes of dust wafted through the air like a million wriggling snakes. She could just about distinguish what had once been her homely, warm owl-hole. Sap spewed across the forest floor, producing an oozing golden blanket. Emma's mother hooted indignantly and shielded her eyes from the piercing sunlight. The creature below swung its blade ferociously, shouting something indistinguishable to the owls' ears.

'Mother, do you think it would be safe to

settle on another tree, in a more secluded part of the forest?' suggested Emma tentatively.

Now that the owls were at a greater height, they noticed numerous other fallen pines scattered throughout the forest. Her mother shook her head apologetically. 'I'm sorry, but I have a dreadful feeling that those foul creatures intend to tear down the whole forest to establish their own territory here,' she spat, 'and I'm afraid there's nothing we can do about that.'

Emma clacked her beak in suspension and suddenly a wave of dreariness sliced through her. 'Mother, I'm tired, I'm not usually up so late, and it's so bright I can hardly see!' she complained.

'Come on dear, let's get along – we need to find somewhere to rest,' her mother said encouragingly, flapping persistently beside Emma to stir the wind beneath her wings.

Emma hooted gratefully and soared alongside her mother as they spiralled away from the shattered forest. When the last of the trees were left behind them, Emma turned to watch the slowly disintegrating forest that she had once called her home. She rose towards the open heavens and gave a desolate hoot of salute which echoed eerily over the settling mist, before swooping down to join her mother as they wheeled off in search of a new life.

*   *   *

Emma shielded her eyes from the flooding drift of snow and urged herself on. Ice-cold specks flecked through her ruffled feathers and her beak chattered as she drove on through the merciless blizzard. 'You can hardly tell whether it's night or day in this frozen world!' Her words were swiftly snatched away by the dashing wind, after a moment of pause, she called out: 'Mother, are you still there?'

'I'm over here, right next to you!' bleated a meek voice.

'We're nearly there! I can feel it in my toes!' cried Emma joyously, casting a quick glance at her solidly frozen talons.

'Where? We're nearly where?' yelled her mother over the wailing gale.

'Why, the Realm of True Owls of course!'

The snow had subsided and Emma could see the stars twinkling merrily above. A swathe of twinkling gems, each unique in its own glittering way. Within the tiny pinpricks of light that were so far, yet seemed so close, she could always draw peace and comfort.

It was Emma who first noticed the slight shimmer in the air that night. It started out as a pulsing and dwindling haze, flickering in and out of existence. The hues gradually convulsed and broadened, waxing and waning in the silent rhythm of the night.

Suddenly, an array of colour unfurled upon the star-swept sky, unleashing its vivid wonder into the frozen world. The owls' eyes sparkled in hushed awe as they witnessed a phenomenon that so many longed to see... and here they were at the very heart of the earth's greatest pride and beauty. The silken blanket writhed across the whispering snow, swishing noiselessly as if splitting time itself in two. And that was when Emma saw it.

'That's it! *That's it!* Can you see it, Mother? True magic in itself!' breathed Emma. For she had found the gateway to the Realm of True Owls and magic it was, indeed.

Hannah Erlebach, aged 11
Leicester High School for Girls, Leicester

'Rosa heard a faint noise through the trees behind her, so she spun round...'

Darcey Bussell

The Stones

by William O'Hara

Rosa heard a faint noise through the trees behind her, so she spun round to see… nothing. Her pace quickened. The sound persisted. Rosa's once-peaceful walk was now a full-scale sprint. There was the noise again, only closer, like a lion waiting for the right moment to pounce and devour its prey. She ran on. Rosa saw the thorns' sheer edges digging into her skin, but felt no pain. However, she had no time for such a minor thing, even though it was more important than she knew…

Whatever was pursuing her was closing in swiftly. Rosa's legs didn't stop working until she came to a pair of unkempt rose bushes. She felt safe here; this place was a haven to her. She looked around her and a melancholy feeling passed through her. This clearing, her place of safety, was lifeless.

The winter chill had spread over this area like a disease, destroying all life in its destructive path. Dead leaves lay everywhere like a million corpses with no one to mourn them. Bare, once-mighty trees stretched up to the sun in vain as a last hope for survival. Rosa felt helpless. She stood there, devastated, in a mass of thorns. Rosa looked for something living, a last vestige of hope, but found nothing. Rosa was silent and listened closely, taking in every sound. Every noise seemed menacing. There was the din again, the loudest it had ever been. Then it dawned on Rosa. The harrowing sound was actually an innocent child's cry. The sound was sweet-toned, like a lullaby. Cautiously, she turned. There, on a rock enveloped in ivy, was the child.

'Thank goodness I have found you,' said the boy. 'My name is Lewis and I am so alone.'

The boy's grimy face was streaked with tears and his hair stuck to his head as if tarred. His clothes struck Rosa as odd, possibly of Victorian style. He wore a shirt made from fine fabric that was now tattered and blood flecked, stained to a sickly brown colour. His leggings were laddered and his trousers slashed.

Rosa took a few steps back and imagined Lewis in a different time and place, she imagined Lewis in brand new clothes, a clean face and spotless hair. 'You were quite a rich boy, weren't you?'

'Yes,' replied Lewis, 'I am a direct descendant

of the Saxon family and I was once a very well-regarded young man, until I ended up in this place.'

'Pleased to make your acquaintance *Sir* Lewis Saxon,' she said mockingly. The boy smiled for, as far as Rosa could tell, the first time in quite a few years. She tried to shake his hand but something happened, something supernatural…

Just as Rosa was about to shake Lewis' hand, a chill ran down her spine. Then it happened. Her flesh passed through his. Rosa shrank back in horror. Lewis' face demonstrated utter confusion. Rosa turned on her heel and ran.

'Wait!' cried Lewis. Tears stung Rosa's eyes. She wanted to go and hug that pitiful boy, but she just couldn't. Rosa knew that she would have to endure guilt's keen sting, but for now her only concern was escaping the ghostly boy.

Days later, guilt and remorse got the better of Rosa. Lewis was just a poor tortured soul – a victim of a merciless enemy known as death. She ran as fast as her legs would carry her, back to the clearing. Rosa felt that warm friendly feeling. Instantly, it was crushed like a delicate rose petal. Lewis wasn't there. Now she could never apologise for her heartless deed. Then, she felt a tingling in the pit of her stomach. She heard Lewis' voice, calling to her. Rosa turned on her heel and followed the voice until she came to a pair of rusting black iron gates. Tentatively, she walked in. There was the voice again. It was coming from the left! Suddenly, grim feelings spread throughout Rosa. She was standing in a graveyard.

She looked around her and thought of all the pain and suffering. It broke her fragile spirit. Then Rosa felt something else, something different. Her feet started walking. She wasn't moving her feet, so who was?

Her body carried her to an ancient part of the graveyard and to one stone in particular. She peered at it. Rosa felt drawn to it. She saw, etched in the weathered granite, the words that made her shake. Rosa understood now.

She read aloud, 'Here lies Rosa Marie. Much loved daughter, Taken from us, St Stephens Day, 1889 AD aged 13. R.I.P.'

It started to rain and her face was wet, though whether by rain or tears, she could not tell.

William O'Hara, aged 10
Brentwood Preparatory School, Essex

The Decision of Eternity

by Reyah Martin

Rosa heard a faint noise through the trees behind her, so she spun round. The noise was hushed and distant like the whisper of the wind. Above Rosa, a thick roof of overlapping trees sheltered the wood and blocked out every chink of sunlight. A tangle of brambles and roots enveloped the ground.

Rosa was fascinated by wildlife and came to the wood every so often to enjoy the peacefulness of the shady trees and relax. This was the safest and most tranquil place Rosa could think of, and all the time she was there she'd fall back onto the soft, green, comfortable moss and just listen to the world around her.

The whispering sound was becoming heavier, like the rustling of autumn leaves. Suddenly, Rosa's heart was drumming in her chest and her eyes were wide with fear, her body besieged with fright. The rustling quickened and the 'Thud! Thud! Thud!' of heavy boots clomped along the forest tracks.

Rosa's breath came in short, fearful gasps. Leaning against the large oak tree, sweat beaded and glistened on her forehead.

A huge hand clamped her mouth shut before she could yell and held it there as the barrel of a gun was pressed against her hot cheek. 'Keep quiet! Or death will take its toll.' His voice was harsh and every noise in the wood could be heard as he took a step closer to her, his breath hot and sharp as it warmed Rosa's skin, hot like sparks of fire. 'I was sent to kill you, you are a danger to the underworld.'

All Rosa could do was watch the man's face. As white as chalk, deeply wrinkled. Leading Rosa to the edge of the dense canopy of weaving trees, he trampled through the brambles and roots and pressed the cool metal of the gun against Rosa's neck, almost preventing the pulse throbbing in her throat.

A crumbling canyon of rock lay behind Rosa, the murderer's face in front of her, purple veins making cutting paths across his face. Torn between thoughts of murder and suicide, Rosa took cautious steps backwards towards the decaying ledge of rock and kept her balance.

Her eyes squeezed tight shut, Rosa stumbled backwards and shoved at the man with all her might.

Falling carelessly as the rock plummeted to the sharp rocks and twigs in the forest beneath her, eyes shut tight, she smashed to the ground beneath the slope and her eyes relaxed but stayed shut. Never to open again....

Reyah Martin, aged 10
St Barbara's Primary School, Glasgow

'My single bed was sometimes a wooden boat'

Carol Ann Duffy

My Monstrous Family

by Oscar Jelley

My single bed was sometimes a wooden boat,
I sail boldly through the stormiest seas,
My first mate is a parrot, who wears an eye patch,
And my cabin dog has itchy fleas.
My chef is a cat, who cooks mouldy steak,
And he's partial to a nice bit of fish,
And I am a captain, who cares for his crew,
And spaghetti is my favourite dish.
We've swashbuckled through the stormiest seas,
We've fought the perilous creature named Dad,
We've outsmarted the stupidity of the big brother,
Oh, what adventures we've had.
We've covered our ears when the siren named
Mum,
Lets out her terrible scream,
When the dragon named Auntie comes to stay,
Her eyes flutter and gleam.
The monster named Sister is hard to bear,
As she sprays out her Perfume of Doom,
While the Cyclopes Granny and Grandad,

Are obsessed with cleaning my room.
There are just two monsters to mention,
Who are the worst out of all that we've seen,
Sea monsters Uncle and Cousin,
Have a threat that is doubly mean.
But all of these monsters aren't that bad,
And there are far worse monsters out there,
And my mission is to seek and stop them,
So follow me if you dare!

Oscar Jelley, aged 10
Manor Field Primary School, West Sussex

Grandma's Bed

by Anna Wasse

My single bed was sometimes a wooden boat
When I was young like you are now
I would sail away in it
My head was leaning on the bow
And I would quietly think and sit
For hours and hours and hours.

Sometimes my single bed was a cubby hole
When I was young and strong like you
Underneath I'd make a den
With Teddy, Rabbie and Mr Seal too
They were my best friends.

When I was young and strong like you.
But now I'm old and cannot walk
My single bed is where I stay
And wait for dreams to come to me
But how I wish that I could play
On my little wooden boat again
And forever sail away.

Anna Wasse, aged 8
Norwich High School for Girls, Norwich

Look out for the Secondary title

FROM THE WORLD BOOK DAY
SHORT STORIES COMPETITION
2010 – 2011

IMAGINATION
STATION
AND OTHER
STORIES AND POEMS

WORLD
BOOK
DAY

www.worldbookday.com

STOP PRESS

Information for our
World Book Day 2011 – 2012
competition will be on our website
<u>www.evansbooks.co.uk</u>
from September 2011.

Register your school to
take part.